CW00996887

Aboriginal American Weaving

by Mary Lois Kissell

Copyright © 10/2/2015
Jefferson Publication

ISBN-13: 978-1517636081

Printed in the United States of America

Wonderful as is the development of modern machinery for the manufacture of American textiles—machinery which seems almost human in the way it converts raw materials into finished cloth; just as surprising are the most primitive looms of the American aborigines, who without the aid of machinery make interesting weavings with only a bar upon which to suspend the warp threads while the human hand completes all the processes of manufacture. Modern man's inventive genius in the textile art has been expended upon perfecting the machinery, while primitive man's ingenuity has resulted in making a beautiful weaving with very simple means.

No doubt could we know the history of primitive loom work in America prior to the coming of the white man, we would find an extended distribution of weaving, but all early textiles have been lost owing to the destructability of the material and the lack of climatic and other conditions suitable for their preservation—conditions such as are present in the hot desert lands of the Southwest and the coast region of Peru. However, so many impressions of weavings have been found on early pottery as to assure us that beautiful work of this kind was made in eastern, middle and southern United States. In western British Columbia at the present time there are tribes carrying on certain forms of weaving which show four interesting types.

FIGURE 1.—KWAKIUTL SQUAW, WEAVING.

The simplest type is the cedar bark mat woven of flat strips in horizontal and vertical lines. In beginning wide strips of the inner bark are hung from their centre over a crossbar of wood which is supported at either end by an upright beam. The halves of the strips hanging in front are then split into strands of the desired width and a line of fine twining woven across to hold them securely. The checker weaving of the mat is now begun at the left edge by doubling the weft element over the last warp and then weaving with the doubled element over and under one warp until the right edge is reached where it is turned back and slipped under an inch of the weaving just completed. Figure 1 shows a squaw at work on such a mat, and when she has completed this half of the mat the second half will be undertaken. She finishes the edge by turning up the warp ends below the last line of weft and binds them with a row of twining just above this last weft.

FIGURE 2.—MAT WITH CHECKED DESIGN.

In their industries, primitive people always utilize the materials found in their environment, because no means is afforded them, as in modern life, for the transportation of materials from a distance. British Columbia is rich in cedar trees, so it is not strange that material from this tree enters so largely into the weaving of this region. Cedar bark lends itself very delightfully to the technic of these mats, and its golden brown checked surface is at times crossed by black lines or broken by a group of black checks in simple designs. These

6

vary greatly, but only one example (Figure 2) can be shown here.

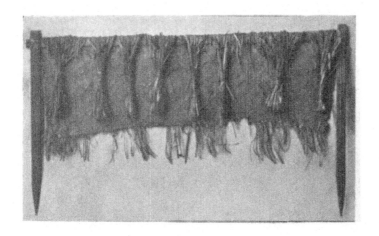

FIGURE 3.—PRIMITIVE LOOM WITH PLAITED MAT.

The second type of weaving, also of cedar bark, is begun like the last mat, but the elements are so placed as to cross the surface diagonally—alternate strips passing diagonally downward to the right and left as in Figure 3. These strips are not woven but plaited over and under each other without the addition of a weft element as in weaving. When the side edge is reached the strips turn over at right angles and continue to plait in the changed oblique direction. The lower edges are finished by bending the elements at right angles and plaiting them obliquely back for an inch into the completed surface. Checked weaving and plaiting is employed in a variety of ways, for aside from mattings it enter into the construction of baskets, pouches, bags, sails, raincoats, baby's hoods, and a number of other articles.

FIGURE 4.—ANOTHER TYPE OF LOOM.

Cedar bark which has been softened and shredded plays an important part in the clothing of this region, especially in blankets like that in Figure 4. The blanket here, however, is not of cedar bark but of goat's hair for a number of materials are made use of by this technic. In this weaving the warps are not thrown over the crossbeam as in the other loom but are supported on a cord which itself is bound to the beam by another cord. Neither are the warps united by a strip of weft running over and under but by a two strand weft element which twines about the warps. To my knowledge this form of weaving has never been reproduced by machinery as no machine can make threads twine. The blankets of cedar bark are undecorated, but those of wool frequently have strands of another color passed across the surface and caught into the weaving from time to time, producing similar designs to that in Figure 4. As observed in the illustration the lines of weft are not driven home but are set some distance apart, the space between varying on different garments. At the lower edge, however, there is frequently found a band of closely woven twining, at other times a band of fur, or a long fringe may complete the edge.

FIGURE 5.—UNFINISHED CHILKAT BLANKET.

The most beautiful weaving of western British Columbia is the Chilkat blanket, Figures 5 and 6, a weaving which is unique in technic and design, both in primitive and modern textile art. It is a ceremonial garment and the gorgeous designs in white, blue, yellow and black are of totemic significance and relate to the ceremonial life of the Indian. In earliest times this blanket was undecorated, a plain field of white; then color was introduced on the white field in stripes of herring-bone pattern typifying raven's tail, because similar to the vanes of the tail feathers; and later the elaborate geometric designs of present day blankets developed. These designs are first painted upon a pattern board the size and shape of those which are to appear upon the blanket, and it is from this pattern board that the squaw weaves her pattern. But although the woman (Figure 7) does weave the blanket, the man also has his part in the process as he furnishes the loom, the pattern board and the skin of the goat. The squaw prepares all the materials and collects the bark, for the warp is of shredded two-ply cedar bark wrapped with a thread of wool, while the weft is entirely of the soft wool of the mountain goat.

FIGURE 6.—OLD CHILKAT BLANKET.

FIGURE 7.—SQUAW WEAVING CHILKAT BLANKET.

Lieut. G. T. Emmons tells us that the goat of this region abounds in the rugged coast mountains from Puget Sound to Cook's Inlet, but is unknown on the outlying islands. Its preference is the glacial belt and snow-fields of the most broken country and the terraced sides of the precipitous cliffs. It is gregarious in habit being found in bands of from ten to fifty or more. From September until April the skin is in prime

12

condition with an abundance of soft wool under a heavy covering of long coarse hair; but the hunting is only done in the autumn. To prepare for the plucking, the skin must be kept wet on the underside so it is moistened and rolled up for several days, thus loosening the hold of the fleece. With thumb and fingers of both hands the squaw, seated upon the ground, pushes the fleece from her, procuring by this process great patches of wool and hair. Then the hairs are plucked out and thrown away and the wool is ready to be spun. During the spinning the woman also sits upon the ground with legs outstretched, with the crude wool by her left side within easy reach. This she draws out with her left hand and feeds to her right, in the amount necessary to form the required size of thread. As it is received between the palm of the right hand and the right thigh, it is rolled from the body and falls to the side in loose, connected thread. This soft thread is next spun between the palm of the hand and the thigh to form a single tightly twisted strand; and by the same process two of these strands are rolled together to form the weft

13

thread for the blanket. In technic the blanket is related to the last one described for it is a twine weaving, but a twilled twine as the two strand weft encloses two warps at a move and with each succeeding line of weft advances one warp giving the surface a twilled effect. It is interesting that the small blocks of design are woven separately something as a tapestry, and later the blocks are sewed together with a thread of sinew from the caribou or whale.

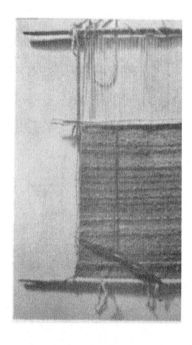

FIGURE 8.—A THIRD   FIGURE 9.—

TYPE OF LOOM. NAVAJO LOOM.

The weaving from this region which most
nearly approaches machine work in process
of making is the dog-hair and goat's wool
blanket. It is woven upon a loom of two
revolving cylindrical beams, supported by
upright posts at either end (Figure 8). The
end of the warp thread is attached to a
staying cord stretched from post to post
about midway between the revolving beams.
The warp then encircles the loom, catches
under the staying cord, then turns and travels
back to its starting point, there to catch
under the staying cord and repeat the
operation. The weft moves across the warps
as in twilled cloth, over two, under two, with
an advance of one warp at each line of weft.
Dog's hair, duck down and goat's wool are
the materials used, especially the latter.
These materials are spun in two-ply thread
twisted partly upon the thigh of the weaver
and finished on a spindle.

Leaving this weaving area in western
British Columbia we pass to the other

locality of note in North America where primitive weaving is practised,—in southwestern United States and northern Mexico. Here the loom work is at a more advanced stage of development than that of the northern area, the weavers making use of a loom frame, sheds, healds, batten and an improvised shuttle. The Navajo Indians are the most skilled weavers north of Mexico and a description of their weaving is fairly typical of this area. As the warps are of soft pliable threads they must of necessity be stretched between two beams. These are suspended vertically if the weaving is to be of any great size, the distance between them being that of the proposed length of the blanket (Figure 9). The warp threads are not stretched across the beams with an oval movement but are laced over them, forming two sheds, the upper of which is held intact by means of the shed-rod, and the lower by a set of healds passing over a heald-rod. A wooden fork serves as a reed and a slender twig as a shuttle. Upon this twig is loosely wound from end to end the weft thread. The shuttle at one move crosses less than half of the warps as the batten—a flat stick of hard oak—is too short to open more than that length of the shed for the passage of the shuttle.

FIGURE 10.—HOPI BLANKET.

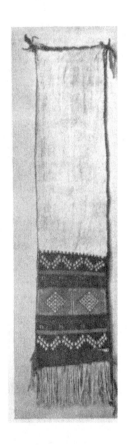

FIGURE 11.—HOPI WEAVING.

FIGURE 12.—MEXICAN SERAPE.

In Figure 10 only a portion of a blanket from the Hopi Indians is shown, that the delicate design may be better seen. A number of Hopi patterns have this fine white line of tracery upon the dark background and it is this play of the fine line pattern on the fabric which is one of the chief beauties of Hopi weavings. The sparkle of white is even more brilliant in Figure 11, another smaller weaving from the same people. They make constant use of the diagonal or twilled technic, a weave which requires that the warps be divided into four sheds, the upper supplied with a shed stick, the three lower with healds. The sheds are shifted in a variety of orders for the construction of different patterns.

FIGURE 13.—HUICHOL WEAVING.

One of the most beautiful weavings the writer has ever seen from the southwest is that pictured in Figure 12, which is, however, only a small center portion of the beautiful serape from Mexico. The pattern in two colors of indigo upon a tan colored ground is especially effective, while the tiny blue dots sprinkled upon the tan surface and the tan dots over the blue design add a subtle and delightful charm not frequently met with.

The last two examples, Figures 13 and 14, are also from Mexico, the first a bit of weaving with animal designs from the Huichol Indians, and the last a belt loom from the same people. In making belts and other narrow fabrics the loom is either horizontal or oblique in position, stretching from some post or tree to the weaver and there attached to a loop which passes either about the waist or under the thighs and rendered tense by the weight of the weaver. These belts may be woven with two or four sheds according to the style of weaving desired, while another method of pattern work on two shed weaving has the addition of a round stick run into the warps so as to raise certain threads while the weft passes two or three times underneath producing a variety of damask weaving.

The stretch between these simple methods of primitive peoples and machine methods of modern life is great indeed and we will long continue to wonder that with such crude devices these people could produce results which compare favorably with our modern weavings.

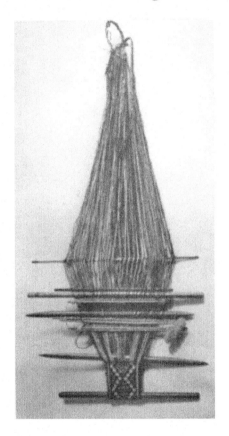

FIGURE 14.—MEXICAN BELT LOOM.

CPSIA information can be obtained at www.ICGtesting.com
Printed in the USA
BVOW06s1851101016

464659BV00012B/115/P